The Goodbye Painting

by Linda Berman, M.A.

Illustrated by Mark Hannon

 HUMAN SCIENCES PRESS, INC.
72 FIFTH AVENUE
NEW YORK, N.Y. 10011

Copyright © 1983 by Linda Berman
Published by Human Sciences Press, Inc.
72 Fifth Avenue
New York, N.Y. 10011
All rights reserved.
Printed in the United States of America
 3456789 987654321

Library of Congress Cataloging in Publication Data

Berman, Linda, 1948–
    The goodbye painting.

    Summary: Nick paints a special picture to express
his feelings when his favorite babysitter moves to
faraway California.
    [1. Baby sitters—Fiction.   2. Painting—Fiction]
I. Hannon, Mark, ill.   II. Title.
PZ7.B4537Go   [E]   LC 81-20217
ISBN 0–89885–074–6   AACR2

To my
Mother and Father

Nick lived in a red brick house across the street from the park. He lived there with his Dad and his dog, Sam, and his best-ever babysitter, Sara.

There had been lots of babysitters. Some were always grouchy and said, "Nick, can't you ever be quiet?" Some were always tired and said, "Nick, can't you ever sit still?"

But Sara was different. Sara remembered things, important things, like cutting the crust off his peanut butter sandwiches, and sending his sneakers to school on gym days. She always waited for the school bus with him and waved goodbye when it came. When he came home from school, she always said, "Hi Nick. Let's see what you made today."

Sara loved to paint, and sometimes when Nick came home from school, they would sit at the kitchen table together and paint pictures. They painted lots of pictures of Sam; he was their most cooperative model. While he snoozed in the corner, they painted picture after picture of Sam in outer space, Sam in a submarine, and Sam exploring mountains and forests.

When Nick got wiggly and didn't feel like sitting still any longer, they went across the street to the park and ran. They ran through the quiet woods full of tall trees that shed soft pine needles on the ground. They ran fast. Sam panted, Sara smiled, and Nick laughed out loud.

One day after school, when Nick and Sam were both thinking about the last chocolate chip cookie on the plate, Sara picked Nick up and sat him on her lap. "I have something important to tell you, Nick," she said. "In a month I'm going to move to California. I'm going back to school."

"You mean you won't be living here anymore?" Nick asked. "No, and that makes me very sad. I'll miss you very much, Nick, and you too, Sam."

Sam thumped his tail on the floor just the way he always did when someone mentioned his name. Nick just sat very still and thought hard about what Sara had said.

As soon as Nick got home from school the next day, Sara said, "I brought a map to show you where California is." They spread it out on the table and Sara made an 'X' to show where she would be living. Then she made another 'X' to show where Nick lived. "California is very far away from here," said Sara.

"It sure is," agreed Nick in a very small voice. Then he asked, "Sara, why do you have to go to school anyway? I think it's a terrible idea."

"Well, Nick, because I want to learn to be an artist. There are teachers there who can help me to become a good painter."

"Who wants to be a painter anyway? Painting is really dumb. I'm never going to paint another picture—especially not with you!" Nick got up and ran out of the kitchen. He slammed the door just as hard as he could and then he slammed it again.

Sara marked the day she would leave on the calendar. She drew a picture of an airplane on a square that said Thursday. Under the airplane she drew a happy face and a sad face. "The happy one is because I'm excited about going back to school, and the sad one is because I'm sorry to be leaving." Looking at the calendar made Nick's stomach hurt, but he didn't say anything about his stomach; instead he shouted, "Well, I'm not sorry you're leaving. You are the worst babysitter ever and I hope you never come back here!"

Ten, nine, eight, that Thursday kept getting closer and closer. Whenever no one was looking, Nick counted off the days left. Then he'd hold up his fingers so Sam could see the bad news for himself. Sam nodded his head and scratched himself thoughtfully the way he always did when someone told him something important.

The night before Sara left, Nick was lying in bed trying to think up ways to stop Sara from going . . . maybe he could tie her up so she'd miss her plane, or hide her suitcase. Then he heard his Dad on the phone saying, "Another babysitter." He put his head far down under the covers and, even though he didn't mean to cry, pretty soon his pillow was all soggy.

The next morning Sara was busy packing, so Nick's Dad made him breakfast. Nick couldn't decide if he wanted eggs or cereal, and then it turned out that there were no eggs, and the only kind of cereal they had was the kind with raisins, and Nick hated raisins.

Right before the school bus came, Sara gave Nick a tight, squashy hug and said, "I promise to write to you and tell you all about California. I hope you write to me too." Nick didn't say anything at all.

At school Nick just couldn't help knocking over Chris' block building, or pushing Ted out of line on the way to the library, or hiding Tricia's new baseball glove under the rug. He had to go sit by himself five times.   It was an awful morning.

Nick missed Sara so much that some days it was hard to think of anything else. Sometimes, though, he would take Sam to the park to run. Then he'd run as hard and fast as he could, and that would feel nice. He wondered if Sara would really write to him, or if she would be too busy the way lots of grown-ups were. He remembered the mean things he said and he wished he could tell her he really didn't mean it.

Ellen, the new sitter, couldn't draw and didn't like to run, but she did make great chocolate chip cookies. After lunch on Saturday Ellen asked Nick if he would like to help her. Nick said, "No, thanks, Ellen." and went to his room.

Sam liked the warm, chocolate smell in the kitchen and stretched himself out right in front of the stove. After a while, Nick thought he'd keep Sam company. Even though he just sat and watched, Ellen let him lick out the bowl and pass it on to Sam. When Sam finished licking out that bowl it was so clean it looked as if it had already been washed. Nick picked up a dish towel and pretended he was drying it.

When Ellen saw what Nick was doing, she laughed and said that she bet Sara missed having two such good helpers around. Nick smiled a little at that, and it felt good, but he didn't let Ellen see him. He wasn't quite ready to be her friend.

Nick had almost given up checking the mail when one day there was a package addressed to him. He knew right away who it was from. He ripped off the brown paper and the strings, and inside was a beautiful box of paints. There was every color in the rainbow and more, and there was a letter that said:

"Dear Nick, I hope you change your mind about painting. California is great, but I miss you and Sam. Your friend, Sara."

Nick was so excited he could hardly wait to start painting. As quickly as he could, he got out his brushes and paper and water. Then he sat down to paint. First, he made the park with the tall, green trees lined up in straight rows. Then he put in Sam, wagging his tail and panting hard. Next, he drew himself, almost as tall as the trees and running fast. And last, he drew Sara wearing her old, paint-spotted, blue tee shirt, and smiling her unforgettable smile. He worked for a long, long time until he had everything just the way he wanted it. Then he put down his paint brush and showed it to Sam.

Sam held his head to one side and gave Nick a curious look. "What we have here," Nick said happily, "is a very special picture—a goodbye picture." And because Sam understood, he wagged his tail extra hard.

Selected Children's Books

By John M. Barrett
OSCAR THE SELFISH OCTOPUS
Illustrated by Joe Servello

DANIEL DISCOVERS DANIEL
Illustrated by Joe Servello

By Terry Berger
I HAVE FEELINGS
Illustrated with

I HAVE F
Illustrated with

By Rose Blue
ME AND
Breaking thro
Illustrated by

By Corinne B
LOSING Y
Illustrated by

By Joan Fassler, Ph.D.
MY GRANDPA DIED TODAY
Illustrated by Stewart Kranz

By Barbara Shook Hazen
TWO HOMES TO LIVE IN
A Child's-Eye View of Divorce
Illustrated by Peggy Luks

IF IT WEREN'T
FOR BENJAMIN
Lick the Icing Spoon)
a Hartman

Ph.D., Litt.D.
ER
WORLD
Kamen

s'' Writer's Collective
SOMETIMES
ildren themselves